SPOTTER'S GUIDE
DOGS

Harry Glover

Illustrated by John Francis
and Andy Martin

Edited by Alastair Smith, Rosamund Kidman Cox and Tim Dowley
Designed by Karen Tomlins and Joanne Kirkby
Digital illustrations by Verinder Bhachu
Cover and series designer: Laura Fearn
Consultant: Hazel Palmer

Cover © Jane Burton; p.1 © Robert Dowling/Corbis;
p.2-3 © Jim Richardson/Corbis; p.5 © Robert Dowling/Corbis;
p.6-7 © Yann Arthus-Bertrand/Corbis; p.56 © Kevin R. Morris/Corbis;
p.58-59 © Joe McDonald/Corbis.

First published in 2001 by Usborne Publishing Ltd.,
Usborne House, 83-85 Saffron Hill, London, EC1N 8RT, England.
www.usborne.com

Printed in Spain

CONTENTS

HOW TO USE THIS BOOK

This book is an identification guide to dog breeds. Take it with you whenever you are likely to see dogs – whether you go out walking, to the park or to a dog show.

Originally, most dog breeds were developed to do a certain job. In this book the breeds are arranged into groups according to the jobs for which they were used.

Next to each picture is a short description of the breed. It tells you where the breed originated, its colouring, temperament and height.

When you spot a breed, make a tick in the circle next to its picture.

There is a chart on pages 62-63. It lists all the breeds featured in this book. When you spot a certain breed, jot down the date that you saw it on the chart. You'll soon build a record of the breeds that you've spotted.

Name of breed	Date
Löwchen	8/6
Lurcher	8/6
Malinois	5/7
Maltese	10/11
Maremma	10/11

Fill in the chart like this.

4

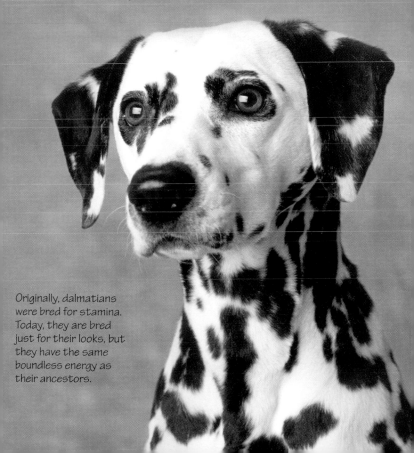

DOG BREEDING

Dogs have been bred for thousands of years – originally to make types that were suited to particular purposes, such as hunting, pulling sledges or guarding. Today's dog breeds started in this way.

Today, dogs are bred more for their beauty than for their qualities as working dogs. However, many retain their ancestors' instincts. For example, a dog that was originally bred to hunt things will tend to chase other animals.

Originally, dalmatians were bred for stamina. Today, they are bred just for their looks, but they have the same boundless energy as their ancestors.

LOOKING AT DOGS

Dogs and their body parts are described with particular words. The most important ones are shown on this picture of a beagle.

Loins

Rump
(croup)

Thigh

Stifle joint
(knee)

Hock

Belly

Chest

Pads
(under
the paw)

HEIGHTS
All dogs' heights are measured from the ground up to the top of the withers. The head is never included.

Crest – the back of the neck

Stop – an indentation between the eyes, where the skull and nose meet.

Muzzle

Withers (top of the shoulders)

Shoulder

Brisket

Elbow

Dew claw

Pastern

DESCRIBING DOGS

Some breeds' features are described in particular ways. Examples include:
• Feathering – long fringes of body hair.
• Racy – slightly built.
• Cobby – heavy, with a short back.
• Stern – the tail of some breeds, such as beagles and foxhounds.
• Wall eyes – eyes of a different colour, for example one blue, one white.

You may hear these terms used by specialists, such as vets, breeders, or judges at dog shows.

7

MARKINGS

Occasionally, the names given to dogs' markings are unusual, and don't give much of a clue as to what the animal's coat really looks like. These pictures explain some of the more unusual names.

Black and tan

Blue

Brindle

Bronze

Buff

Chestnut

Grizzle

Harlequin

Liver

Merle and white

Mouse-grey

Pied

Roan

Salt and pepper

Tricolour

Wheaten

TAILS

When you are identifying breeds, look at the tails. Some breeds hold theirs in a distinctive way, as shown here.

Tails come in all shapes and sizes. However, you may see some dogs with short tails, which have been surgically removed. This is called docking. It is done when the puppy is very young. The argument in favour of docking is that long tails left on working dogs are often injured when the animal is working. Today, though, docking is mostly done for fashion reasons.

Carried upright

Curled

Set high

Set low

Long, flowing

EARS

Dogs' distinctive ears can help you to identify them. However, in some countries the natural shape of the ear is altered by removing part of it so that the remaining part sticks up. This operation is called cropping. In some countries it is illegal.

Erect

Semi-erect

Pendent (hanging)

PEDIGREE

If a dog has ancestors of the same breed, which have been recorded for at least three generations, it is classed as a pedigree dog. Pedigree dogs have been bred for centuries, especially in the Far East and Middle East. Today, they are bred all over the world.

Pedigree registration is controlled by organizations such as kennel clubs. Pedigree breeders usually register puppies soon after they are born. If you buy a pedigree puppy, make sure that you are given its pedigree history, written on an official certificate, when you take it home.

Family tree of a pedigree Dalmatian

Dalmatian grandparent   Dalmatian grandparent   Dalmatian grandparent   Dalmatian grandparent

Dalmatian parent   Dalmatian parent

This dog can produce pedigree dalmatians

CROSS-BRED DOGS

If a dog's parents are of different breeds then it is called a cross-bred dog. For example, if the father is a Golden Retriever and the mother is a German Shepherd, the dog is a Golden Retriever-German Shepherd cross.

Family tree of a cross-bred dog

Golden Retriever   German Shepherd

Cross-bred dog

MONGREL DOGS

A mongrel is a dog of mixed breed whose parents are either not known, or are themselves cross-bred or mongrel.

Family tree of a mongrel

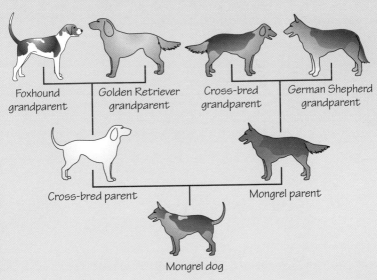

Foxhound grandparent   Golden Retriever grandparent   Cross-bred grandparent   German Shepherd grandparent

Cross-bred parent   Mongrel parent

Mongrel dog

TYPES OF DOG

GUARD DOGS

These dogs were originally bred to guard people and property. Some of them were used for hunting, too. They come from many parts of the world.

Boxer

HERDING DOGS

These dogs were bred to herd other animals – usually sheep or cattle. They were also used as guard dogs. Many are still used for herding in their places of origin.

Border Collie

GUN DOGS

Gun dogs were bred to help hunters. Some are used to find and chase out animals for hunters to shoot. Others are taught to fetch shot animals, usually birds.

Cocker Spaniel

HEELING DOGS

These little dogs were bred to drive cattle. If the cattle stop, the dogs nip their heels, then back off before the animal can kick. This is how they get their name.

Pembroke Corgi

RUNNING DOGS
Running dogs were bred to chase game. Different types have been bred all over the world, but they all share certain traits: they all have long legs, they are lightly built and they can run very fast.

Whippet

HAULING DOGS
These dogs were specially bred to pull sledges over snow and ice in the Arctic. Many are now popular pets. Some are still used to pull sledges for sport and fun.

Alaskan Malamute

SCENT HUNTERS
These dogs have a good sense of smell, which they use to hunt prey. In their home countries they are popular for hunting.

Wire-haired Dachshund

COMPANION DOGS
Dogs of this type were originally bred for a variety of uses. Their small size and friendliness made them popular as pets.

Pekingese

HUNTING TERRIERS
Hunting terriers were bred to chase animals such as foxes, badgers and rats.

Dandie Dinmont Terrier

13

GUARD DOGS

➡ KEESHOND
From Netherlands. Originally used to guard barges, so also called Dutch Barge Dog. Good companion. Fox-like head, and neck ruff. Long coat. Grey, with cream legs and feet. 40-48cm.

"Spectacle" markings around eyes

Feathering on thighs

⬅ SCHIPPERKE
From Belgium. Also called Belgian Barge Dog. Loyal. Short, smooth coat, longer on neck. Usually black. 30-33cm.

➡ BULLDOG
British breed. Brave and determined. Once used for bull baiting. Big head for body. Friendly. Good watchdog. Short coat. Any colour, except black. 31-36cm.

Legs wide apart

➜ BOXER

German breed. Very strong and active. Good guard, but fine house pet, too. Short, smooth coat. Can be red, fawn or brindle, often with white markings. 53-60cm.

The stop is very prominent

Docked tail

Big square head with prominent stop

← BULLMASTIFF

British, bred from Bulldog and Mastiff. Lively, loyal and fearless. Short coat. Red, fawn or brindle. 61-68cm.

➜ ROTTWEILER

German. Used by police and armed forces. Intelligent but strong willed. Short coat. Black and tan. 56-68cm.

GUARD DOGS

➡ GREAT DANE
First used in Germany,
France and Denmark,
to hunt wild boar.
Large but friendly. Will
guard. Short, smooth
coat. Fawn, black,
blue, brindle, or
harlequin. 73-81cm.

Drooping, pendent
ears are cropped
in North America

Tail
held
low

Docked tail

⬅ DOBERMANN
German. Brave and loyal.
Needs training. Short
coat. Black, brown
or blue with tan
markings. 66-68cm.

Ideally, the spots
should not overlap

➡ DALMATIAN
Thought to be
from Dalmatia,
Croatia. Lively and
friendly. Needs lots of
exercise. Short, sleek
coat. White, with black
or liver spots. 55-60cm.

➡ ANATOLIAN KARABASH

From Turkey, where it was first used to guard sheep. Good guard, but needs training. Short coat. Cream, fawn, brindle or black. 66-76cm.

⬅ LEONBERGER

Rare German breed. Friendly house dog and brave guard. Long, softish coat. Golden to red. 68-78cm.

➡ ESTRELA MOUNTAIN DOG

From Estrela mountains, Portugal. Rare. Strong, intelligent and active. Usually fawn, black mask. 63-71cm.

17

GUARD DOGS

➡ NEWFOUNDLAND
From Newfoundland, Canada. Good swimmer. Very strong, but gentle and friendly. Long coat. Black or bronze. 66-71cm.

Pendent ears

Thick coat protects against bad weather

Large head with square muzzle

◀ ST BERNARD
Bred by St Bernard Hospice, Switzerland, to rescue travellers lost in snow. Heavy, strong but gentle. Rough or smooth coat. Usually red and white. 66-71cm.

➡ BERNESE MOUNTAIN DOG
From Switzerland. Was used to pull carts. Easy to train. Long, soft coat. Black, brown or tan markings, white chest. 61-66cm.

The ears are normally pendent, but this dog's are cropped

➡ GIANT SCHNAUZER
From Bavaria, Germany, where it was used to herd cattle. Energetic. Good guard dog, but needs training. Wiry coat. Black or salt and pepper. 71cm.

Beard and whiskers

Pendent ears

Bushy eyebrows

Docked tail

Beard and whiskers

⬅ STANDARD SCHNAUZER
From Bavaria, Germany. Once used to kill rats and other pests. Lively, keen watch dog. Needs training. Wiry coat. Black or salt and pepper. 45-51cm.

This dog's ears have been cropped

Beard and whiskers

Docked tail

➡ MINIATURE SCHNAUZER
From Bavaria, Germany. Loyal, active and alert. Rough, hard coat. Black or salt and pepper. 30-45cm.

GUN DOGS

➡ WELSH SPRINGER SPANIEL
Originally from Wales. Smaller than English Springer. Used for fetching shot birds from water. Lively, energetic pet. Straight, thick, silky coat. Red and white. 45-48cm.

Docked tail

⬅ ENGLISH SPRINGER SPANIEL
Old spaniel breed. Finds, drives out and retrieves game. Active. Needs regular exercise. Usually liver and white, or black and white. 51cm.

➡ IRISH WATER SPANIEL
Old breed. Good at retrieving game from water. Playful and active. Stiff, short curly coat. Dark liver colour. 51-58cm.

Top-knot of curly hair

Short, smooth tail tip

➡ COCKER SPANIEL

British. Very popular show dog and pet. Intelligent, but needs lots of exercise. Longish coat. Many colours, such as black, red, liver or golden. 38-49cm.

Long, drooping, pendent ears

Stop

Long, drooping, pendent ears

⬅ AMERICAN COCKER SPANIEL

Smaller than English Cocker. Lively. Coat feathered on body and legs. Thick coat needs regular grooming. Buff, black, or mixed colours. 34-39cm.

Long, drooping, pendent ears

➡ FIELD SPANIEL

British. Friendly. Shorter legs, longer body than other Spaniels. Medium length coat. Most often black, red, liver or roan. 45cm.

GUN DOGS

➡ SUSSEX SPANIEL

From England. Rare. Active, friendly and very easy to train. Heavy body, with short legs. Always liver, with gold tips. 38-40cm.

Docked tail

Docked tail

Long, heavy body

Short legs

⬅ CLUMBER SPANIEL

From Clumber Park, England. Strong and friendly. Heavy, with short legs. Close, silky coat. White with lemon markings. 48-51cm.

Long, wavy coat

Long tail

➡ SMALL MÜNSTERLANDER

From Westphalia, Germany. Used for finding and retrieving game. Friendly. White and brown, with roan marks. 48-56cm.

Deep chest

➡ CHESAPEAKE BAY RETRIEVER

Originally from East coast of USA. Intelligent, but strong willed and needs training. Dark brown to faded tan. 53-66cm.

Short, slightly wavy coat

⬅ LABRADOR RETRIEVER

From Newfoundland, Canada, and named after Labrador, a region there. Popular gun dog, guide dog, police dog and pet. Black, chocolate or golden. 54-57cm.

Short, thick coat

➡ CURLY-COATED RETRIEVER

British working dog. Strong gun dog. Can retrieve from water. Active, intelligent. Black or liver colour. 63-68cm.

Tightly curled coat

23

GUN DOGS

➡ FLAT-COATED RETRIEVER
British. Good retrieving dog.
Strong and intelligent. Playful
pet. Black or liver colour.
51-61cm.

Flat, springy
coat

Feathering
on tail and thighs

Feathering
on front legs

Flat or wavy coat
with feathering

⬅ GOLDEN RETRIEVER
Popular British breed.
Works well. Good house
dog, but needs lots of
exercise. Any shade
of cream or gold.
51-61cm.

Docked tail

➡ WEIMARANER
From Weimar,
Germany. Friendly,
alert and active.
Smooth coat. Silvery
mouse-grey colour.
56-63cm.

Very short,
fine coat

➡ ENGLISH SETTER
Old British breed. Good family pet. Black and white, lemon and white, liver and white, or tricolour. 61-68cm.

Stop

Feathering on legs and tail

Long, silky, slightly wavy coat

⬅ GORDON SETTER
Originally from Scotland. Heavy breed. Loyal, but tricky to train. Long, soft and glossy coat. Shiny black with tan markings. 66cm.

Stop

➡ IRISH SETTER
From Ireland. Works well when trained. Very lively. Long neck and head. Long, silky coat. Always chestnut. 61cm.

Deep chest

25

GUN DOGS

➡ VIZSLA
From Hungary. Finds and retrieves shot game birds. Gentle and affectionate, though very active. Short coat. Sandy yellow. 57-64cm.

Long, drooping, pendent ears

Short, glossy coat

⬅ POINTER
Originally from Spain. Points at game bird with nose, body and tail in straight line. Very active. Black, or another colour with white. 61-68cm.

Docked tail

➡ GERMAN SHORT-HAIRED POINTER
Finds and retrieves game. Friendly, but needs lots of exercise. Good guard. Liver, or liver and white spotted or flecked. 63-66cm.

Short, hard coat

➡ **DRENTSE PATRIJSHOND**
From Netherlands. Good
at hunting partridge.
Will fetch game from
water. Thick, longish
coat. White, with
brown or orange.
56-63cm.

Feathered
ears

Long,
feathered
tail

Fairly smooth coat

⬅ **BRITTANY SPANIEL**
Originally from Brittany,
France. Fast, intelligent.
Good pet. White, with
brown or orange.
45-51cm.

Ears hang
flat

➡ **LARGE MÜNSTERLANDER**
From Germany. Good
gun dog and pest
catcher. Active.
Needs training.
White with black
patches. 58-63cm.

Long,
slightly
wavy coat

27

HERDING DOGS

➡ MAREMMA
From Central Italy.
Good herder and
guard. Intelligent,
though independent.
Black nose. Usually
white, can have
lemon or fawn
markings. 61-74cm.

Longish coat

Long
neck hair

Long
neck
hair

Short, wavy
body hair

⬅ KUVASZ
From Hungary. Used
for guarding sheep
and cattle. Loyal and
protective. Always
white. 67-76cm.

Thick coat

**⬅ PYRENEAN
MOUNTAIN DOG**
From Pyrenees
mountains on the
French-Spanish border.
Guards sheep. Large
and strong, though
gentle. All white, or
white with markings.
66-81cm.

➡ GROENENDAEL

Sheepdog from Belgium.
Intelligent and obedient.
Very good watch dog.
Fairly long coat. Black.
58-62cm.

Triangular, erect ears

Long neck hair

Triangular, erect ears

⬅ MALINOIS

Belgian Shepherd Dog.
Smooth coat, similar to
German Shepherd Dog.
Fawn or red colouring,
with black hair tips.
58-62cm.

➡ TERVUEREN

From Belgium. Looks like
Groenendael, but is
reddish-fawn with black
hair tips and tail tip.
58-62cm.

HERDING DOGS

➡ GERMAN SHEPHERD DOG
Used by police, armed
forces and as guide dog
for blind. Intelligent,
loyal and easy to
train. Any colour.
56-66cm.

Triangular,
erect ears

Tail hangs in
slight curve

Smooth
coat

Long outer
coat

Full neck
ruff

Semi-erect
ears

⬅ ROUGH COLLIE
Originally from Scotland,
where it was used to herd
sheep. Friendly and active.
Needs regular grooming.
Usually sable and white, blue
and white or tricolour. 61-68cm.

➡ SMOOTH COLLIE
British. Less common
than Rough Collie.
Has a short,
smooth, hard
coat. 51-61cm.

Semi-erect
ears

➡ OLD ENGLISH SHEEPDOG

Often called "bobtail". Good guard dog. Strong and active. Needs daily grooming. Grey, blue or grizzle, with or without white. Over 56cm.

Ears lie flat on head

No tail

⬅ BEARDED COLLIE

Originally from Scotland. Mainly used as sheepdog. Loyal, loving pet. Long coat. Can be blue, grey-black, red and white. 51-56cm.

Beard on both sides of muzzle

➡ SHETLAND SHEEPDOG

Originally from Shetland Islands, Scotland. Looks like small Rough Collie. Ideal family pet. Colours include black and white, black and tan, merle, sable. 35-37cm.

Semi-erect ears

Full neck ruff

31

HERDING DOGS

➡ TIBETAN TERRIER
From mountains of Tibet.
Once used to herd sheep,
goats and cattle. Lively,
active and intelligent. Long,
fine double coat. White,
cream, grey, golden and
black. 35-40cm.

Tail curled
over back

Large, round feet

Tail curled
over back

Corded coat

⬅ PULI
From Hungary. Woolly
undercoat. Long outer
coat hangs in cords and
needs regular attention.
Can work in cold
conditions. White, grey
or black. 38-44cm.

➡ KOMONDOR
From Hungary. Thick coat
hangs in long cords.
Bold, hard worker.
Loyal, protective
companion. Always
white. 56-81cm.

Curved tail

Corded
coat

Hair falls
over eyes

➡ BORDER COLLIE
Good working sheepdog, from northern England. Very intelligent and energetic. Needs regular, hard exercise. Longish, smooth or slightly wavy coat. Usually black and white. 51-53cm.

Eyebrows hang over eyes

⬇ BRIARD
French breed. Intelligent and active. Square look to body. Can be any colour apart from white. 56-58cm.

Feathered, curved tail

Docked tail

➡ BOUVIER DES FLANDRES
Bred in Flanders, Belgium, to herd cattle. Active. Rough, wiry coat. Has eyebrows, beard and moustache. Drab yellow, grey or black. 59-68cm.

HEELING DOGS

➡ KELPIE
Australian. Bred from
sheepdogs. Hard working.
Tough and active. Short
coat. Black, red
or chocolate.
43-51cm.

Erect
ears

Tail curled
over back and
to one side

⬅ NORWEGIAN BUHUND
Farm dog. Brave and
intelligent. Long, thick coat,
which is longest on body
and neck. Fawn, red
or yellowish. 45cm.

Speckled
coat

➡ AUSTRALIAN CATTLE DOG
Bred from Smooth Collie,
dingo (wild dog) and
Dalmatian. Tough. Used for
driving cattle. Short coat.
Red or blue speckled.
45-51cm.

34

➡ VALLHUND

From Sweden. Also called "Västgötaspets". Almost died out in 1940s. Has short coat. Can be grey, brownish or red. 38-49cm.

Very short tail

Erect ears

Short coat

Very short tail

⬅ PEMBROKE CORGI

Originally used to drive cattle and ponies in South Wales. Now a popular pet. Will nip. Can be red, black, fawn, black or tan. Can have white markings. 25-30cm.

Large, erect ears point out

➡ CARDIGAN CORGI

Another driving dog from South Wales. Longer body and larger ears than Pembroke. Short coat. Will nip. Any colour except all-white. 30cm.

Tail looks like fox's brush

RUNNING DOGS

➡ SALUKI
Bred in Middle East to hunt deer and antelope. Loyal and active. Long ears. White, golden, black and tan. 58-71cm.

Smooth coat

Feathered, curved tail

Feathered legs

⬅ SLOUGHI
Bred in North Africa to hunt small game. Rare. Looks like smooth Saluki. Active. Usually sandy, can be brindle. 56-76cm.

Feathered tail

➡ BORZOI
Bred in Russia to hunt game and wolves. Active and friendly. Various colours. 69-79cm.

Long, silky coat

Long tail, curved at tip

⬅ AFGHAN HOUND
Bred in Afghanistan to hunt deer. Long, silky coat, feathered ears. All colours. 64-74cm.

➡ IRISH WOLFHOUND

Irish breed. One of largest breeds. Good natured. Rough, hard coat. Grey, brindle, red, fawn, black or pure white. Over 71cm.

⬅ DEERHOUND

Scottish breed. Smaller and lighter than Irish Wolfhound. Once used to hunt deer. Thick, rough coat. Grey, yellowish or brindle. 71-76cm.

➡ PHARAOH HOUND

Ancient breed. Probably North African. Smooth coat. Often rich red, with white on chest. 53-63cm.

Large, erect ears

⬅ IBIZAN HOUND

From island of Ibiza, Spain. Used as hunter and watch dog. Rough or smooth coat. 61-66cm.

RUNNING DOGS

➡ GREYHOUND

Ancient breed, used for hunting hares and rabbits. Very fast. Will chase small animals. Now used for track racing. Smooth coat. Most colours. 71-76cm.

Long, low-set tail

Deep chest

⬅ LURCHER

Gypsies' traditional hunting dog. Usually greyhound-collie cross. Rough coated. Fawn, grey or black. 71-76cm.

➡ WHIPPET

Originally from northern England. Bred for racing. Looks like miniature greyhound. Friendly. Smooth coat. Any colour or colour mix. 44-51cm.

Semi-erect ears fold back

Curved back

Semi-erect ears folded back

Arched back

⬅ ITALIAN GREYHOUND

Originally from Italy. Smallest running dog. Quiet and friendly. Smooth coat. Fawn, black, cream, white, pied. 32-35cm.

HAULING DOGS

➡ ALASKAN MALAMUTE

From northern Canada. Large, strong dog. Loves people, but can be aggressive to other dogs. Grey to black, white under body. 58-71cm.

Mask-like markings on head

Thick coat

Tail curves over back

⬅ SIBERIAN HUSKY

From Siberia, northern Russia. Used for herding, sledge pulling. Good worker. Friendly pet. Long, thick, soft coat. All colours, with white markings. 51-59cm.

Small, erect ears

Tail curves over back

➡ SAMOYED

Russian breed. Still used in sledge races. Can round up reindeer. Good pet. Silver-white. May have cream marks. 45-53cm.

Long coat

SCENT HUNTERS

➡ FINNISH SPITZ

Originally from Finland, where it was used for hunting. Good guard. Noisy. Longish coat. Red-gold to red-brown. 39-44cm.

Erect, pointed ears

Tightly-curled tail

⬅ ELKHOUND

Originally from Norway, where it was used to hunt elk. Can stand cold weather. Independent, energetic. Thick, hard coat. Grey. 47-52cm.

Ridge of hairs on back

➡ RHODESIAN RIDGEBACK

From Rhodesia (now Zimbabwe), Africa. Used for guarding and hunting. Strong fighter. Short, glossy coat. Yellowish to reddish. 61-68cm.

➡ BASSET GRIFFON VENDÉEN

From south-west France, where it was used for hunting hares. Active. Mostly white, with markings. 34-43cm.

Long ears

Longish coat

Tail carried high

⬅ BEAGLE

English breed. Originally used for hunting. Active. Very friendly pet. Short, hard coat. Various colours. 34-40cm.

➡ BASSET HOUND

French breed. Good natured. Lively. Smooth, short coat. Various colours. 33-38cm.

Very long, pendent ears

➡ BASENJI

From central Africa. Originally used to hunt antelope. Very friendly. Black, red, chestnut and white, or black and tan with white. 40-43cm.

Tail tightly curled

SCENT HUNTERS

➡ BLOODHOUND

Ancient breed, from Normandy, northern France. Great sense of smell. Used to hunt deer and track scent of escaped prisoners. Short, glossy coat. Black or liver and tan, sometimes red. 61-66cm.

Very long, pendent ears

Loose skin on head

Long tail

⬅ FOXHOUND

Used in packs for hunting, especially in Britain. Friendly. Short, smooth coat. Usually tan, with black and white markings, or white with black, tan or lemon marks. 53-63cm.

➡ OTTERHOUND

British breed, originally to hunt otters. Swims well. Longish, hard coat. Usually fawn or grey with black and tan markings. 61-66cm.

➡ SMOOTH-HAIRED DACHSHUND

Originated in Germany. Once used to pursue badgers underground. Also used to hunt in packs. Short, smooth coat. Any colour but white. 13-23cm.

Long, pendent ears

Breast bone sticks out

⬇ LONG-HAIRED DACHSHUND

Bred for sport, but also very popular as pet. Silky, longish coat. Brown, red, black and tan or dapple colour. 13-23cm.

Feathered body and tail

⬇ WIRE-HAIRED DACHSHUND

Has been used to hunt wild boar and follow other game underground. Short coat. All colours. 13-23cm.

Eyebrows

Feathered body and tail

Beard

COMPANION DOGS

➡ CHOW CHOW
Originally bred in China. Popular pet. Looks a little like a lion. Alert and independent. Black, red, blue, fawn or cream in colour. 46-56cm.

Very thick coat

Tail curls over hip

⬅ PUG
From China. Was popular with English royal family in 1800s. Very loving pet. Short, glossy coat. Fawn or black. 33cm.

➡ LÖWCHEN
Probably comes from the Mediterranean. Also called "Little Lion Dog". Ancient, rare breed. Long coat. Friendly. Usually black, white, grey or cream. 25cm.

Tufted tail

Clipped coat

Crest of hair

⬅ CHINESE CRESTED DOG
Despite its name, probably from Mexico or Africa, not China. Almost hairless. Patches of pink, blue, mauve or white. 33cm.

➡ KING CHARLES SPANIEL
Favourite at court of King
Charles II of England. Gentle
and loving. Long, silky coat.
Black and tan, rich
red or tricolour. 25-27cm.

Short
muzzle

Long,
feathered
ears

⬅ CAVALIER KING CHARLES SPANIEL
Long, silky coat. Larger
than King Charles Spaniel.
Friendly. Black and tan, red
and white, red or tricolour.
31-33cm.

➡ TIBETAN SPANIEL
First bred by monks
of Tibet. Looks like
a Pekingese. Long,
smooth coat. Golden,
cream, white, black,
or tricolour. 24-28cm.

Curled tail

⬅ BICHON FRISE
Probably from Spain.
Friendly. Silky white coat,
often with grey patches
on skin. 20-30cm.

COMPANION DOGS

Rounded
skull

➡ JAPANESE CHIN
Probably originated in China,
but became the pet of
many Japanese emperors.
Long coat. White with red
or black patches. 30cm.

⬅ PAPILLON
First bred in France. Called
"Butterfly Dog" because of
shape of its head and ears.
Long coat. White with all
colours except liver. 28cm.

Tail lies flat
over back

➡ POMERANIAN
From Pomerania,
Germany/Poland. Small
version of Finnish Spitz.
Red, blue, orange, white,
black or brown. 28cm.

⬅ AFFENPINSCHER
Tiny dog, from Germany.
Often shown in old Dutch
paintings. Looks a little like
a monkey. Wiry coat,
usually black. Up to 28cm.

➡ SHIH TZU
Originally from China. Tiny but brave. Rounded skull, square muzzle. Playful. Long straight coat. All colours. Up to 27cm.

Beard and whiskers

Tail curls over back

⬅ MALTESE
Very old breed, from Malta. Often painted in pictures as lap dog. Loyal. Short body and legs. Long, pure white coat. 20-25cm.

➡ PEKINGESE
Originally from China, where it was once a court pet. Long coat. Stubborn. All colours except liver. 15-25cm.

Tail curled over back

⬅ LHASA APSO
Originally from Tibet. Lively and assertive. Long, hard coat. Usually golden, sandy or grey. 25-28cm.

COMPANION DOGS

➡ AUSTRALIAN SILKY TERRIER
Bred in Australia from Yorkshire and Australian Terriers. Long, silky coat. Silver, or blue with tan marks. 22cm.

Small, erect ears

Very long coat with parting in middle

⬅ YORKSHIRE TERRIER
Tiny English Terrier. Very popular pet. Good rat and mouse catcher. Long, straight, silky coat. Should be dark blue and tan coloured. 18-20cm.

➡ GRIFFON BRUXELLOIS
Originally from Belgium. Lively little dog. Rough, wiry, short coat. Red, black or black and tan. 18-20cm.

Docked tail

Heavy whiskers

➡ GRIFFON BRABANÇON
From Belgium. Similar to Griffon Bruxellois, but smooth-coated. Also called "Smooth Griffon". 18-20cm.

Docked tail

➡ CHIHUAHUA, SMOOTH-COAT

Mexican. Smallest breed. Also called "Ornament Dog" or "Pillow Dog". Bold. Can be aggressive. Fine coat. 15-23cm.

Flattish tail

⬅ CHIHUAHUA, LONG-COAT

Silky coat with feathering. Same stature and character as smooth-coated version. Can be any colour. 15-23cm.

➡ POODLES

Probably originated in Germany. Easy to train. Coat curly, hard and thick. Any colour. Split into categories: "Toy", "Miniature" and "Standard". Category sizes vary according to different rules of various kennel clubs around the world.

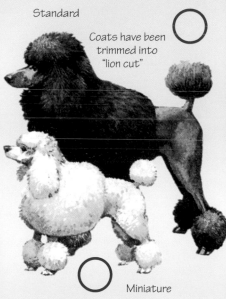

Standard

Coats have been trimmed into "lion cut"

Miniature

Toy

COMPANION DOGS

➡ FRENCH BULLDOG
Has large ears, which look like a bat's. Very friendly little dog. Short coat. Brindle, fawn or pied. 26-35cm.

Docked tail

White collar

⬅ BOSTON TERRIER
Originally from the USA. Lively and clever. Short, glossy coat. Broad, round head. Brindle and white, or black and white. 40cm.

➡ ENGLISH TOY TERRIER
Also called "Black and Tan". Miniature version of Manchester Terrier. Brave and alert. Good rat hunter. Smooth, short coat. Black and tan. 25-30cm.

Docked tail

⬅ MINIATURE PINSCHER
German breed. Lively and spirited, but easily trained. Short, smooth coat. Red, black, blue or chocolate with tan markings. 25-30cm.

HUNTING TERRIERS

➡ MANCHESTER TERRIER
Originally from Manchester,
northern England, where
it was used to catch rats.
Intelligent and lively. Short,
glossy coat. Black and tan.
38-40cm.

Short, glossy coat

Egg-shaped
head

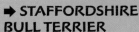

⬅ BULL TERRIER
English breed. Friendly
to people, but fights dogs.
Short, smooth coat. White,
sometimes with markings,
or coloured. 35-40cm.

Semi-erect
ears

**➡ STAFFORDSHIRE
BULL TERRIER**
From Staffordshire, England.
Short, glossy coat. Very friendly
with people, but loves to fight
other dogs. Red, fawn, blue
or black. 36-41cm.

⬅ JACK RUSSELL TERRIER
British. Bred from several
different types of terrier.
Excellent pest catcher. Short
or rough coated. White with
coloured patches. 23-38cm.

Short
legs

HUNTING TERRIERS

➡ WEST HIGHLAND TERRIER

Originally from Scotland. Popular house pet. Good guard. Long, coarse coat, soft undercoat. Always white. Up to 28cm.

Small, upright tail

⬅ SCOTTISH TERRIER

Once called "Aberdeen Terrier". Show dog and pet. Intelligent. Wiry, longish coat. Black, flecked grey or brown. 25-28cm.

➡ SEALYHAM TERRIER

Originally from Wales, where it was used for hunting in packs. Long, wiry coat. White, sometimes with yellow markings on head and ears. 30cm.

Slightly curved head

➡ CAIRN TERRIER

Originally from Scotland. Similar to West Highland. Longish, hardish coat. Red, sandy, grey, mottled brown or off-black. 24-26cm.

Small, pointed, erect ears

➡ NORWICH TERRIER AND NORFOLK TERRIER

British breeds, very similar to one another. Norwich has erect ears, Norfolk has semi-erect ears. Wiry coat. Red, black and tan, sandy or greyish colour. 25cm.

Docked tail

Erect ears

⬅ BORDER TERRIER

Very active breed. Rough, weatherproof coat. Red, wheaten, grey and tan or blue and tan colour. 26-30cm.

➡ DANDIE DINMONT TERRIER

Named after character in a book by Sir Walter Scott. Coat of mixed soft and hard hairs. Pepper or mustard colour. 20-28cm.

Large, wide head

Docked tail

⬅ AUSTRALIAN TERRIER

Popular in Australia and New Zealand. Strong and friendly. Hard, straight coat. Red, or blue and tan in colour. 25cm.

HUNTING TERRIERS

➡ AIREDALE TERRIER
Named after Aire Valley, Yorkshire, England. Largest terrier. Bred to hunt pests. Srong but easy to train. Rough, wiry coat. Black or grey and tan. 55-61cm.

⬅ LAKELAND TERRIER
From northern England. Used for hunting. Friendly. Rough, thick coat. Various colours. 37cm.

➡ WELSH TERRIER
Used in Wales to hunt. Strong. Good guard dog and house dog. Hard, wiry coat. Black and tan. 39cm.

Semi-erect ears carried forward

Beard and whiskers

Beard and whiskers

⬅ KERRY BLUE TERRIER
Irish. Bred to hunt fox, badger and otter. Popular show dog. Friendly, but fights. Soft wavy coat. Any blue shade. 46-48cm.

➡ IRISH TERRIER

From Ireland. Likes to fight, but friendly to people. Fairly short coat. Any shade of red. 45cm.

Semi-erect ears

Short, wiry coat

Top knot

Arched back

⬅ BEDLINGTON TERRIER

From northern England. Looks a little like a lamb. Brave and friendly. Good pet. Thick, wavy coat. Blue, liver, sandy or mixed colours. 40cm.

➡ FOX TERRIER, SMOOTH-COAT

From England. Lively and intelligent. Short, hard, smooth coat. Mainly white. 37-39cm.

Short back

Tapering head

Short back

Long, square muzzle

⬅ FOX TERRIER, WIRE-COAT

Similar to Smooth-coat, but with longer, wiry hair. White, some black or tan markings. 37-39cm.

CHOOSING A DOG

Dogs can be fantastic companions, and great fun. However, they need a lot of looking after. Make sure that you will be able to commit lots of time and energy to looking after your dog.

Find out as much as you can about the different breeds. Choose a dog that is the right size and temperament to suit your lifestyle.

PUPPIES

Choose a puppy that is friendly to you. However, beware of any that are too bold, they may be hard to train. Similarly, watch out for very shy ones, they may stay nervous all their lives.

If you want to buy a puppy, look for signs that it is healthy. The picture below shows some of the things to look for.

Check that the coat is healthy. A poor coat can be a sign of hard-to-treat skin problems.

Inspect the ears. Dirty ears are a clue that the pup may be ill.

Bright eyes are a sign of good general health.

Look for a full set of teeth. Bad teeth may signal illness.

DOG CARE

Grooming keeps your dog's skin healthy, and helps to get rid of any shed hairs. Get your puppy used to being groomed as soon as possible, so that the job is easy and stress free for both of you.

Dogs over six months old should be bathed every few months, unless they are very dirty. Use a dog shampoo, and dry the dog with a towel reserved just for its own use. Drying will prevent your pet from catching a chill.

EQUIPMENT

• A metal comb, for long-haired dogs. Start grooming with this, to remove tangles and dirt.

• A hound glove. For smooth-coated dogs. The bristle side is for brushing, the velvet side for finishing off.

• A bristle brush, for long-haired dogs. Use this after you have finished with the metal comb.

• Coat clippers. These are for dogs that need special clipping, such as a poodles or schnauzers.

• A two-sided brush. The metal bristles are to clean and untangle hair. The nylon bristles are for finishing off.

• Nail clippers. Only use these if you have been shown how.

TRAINING - THE BASICS

The ancestors of domestic dogs lived in packs with a leader dog. Your dog will see you as its leader and will expect to obey you. Training is therefore very important. If it is done with patience and care the dog will enjoy being trained. You should start from the day your dog comes to live with you.

Remember that a dog can't understand what you are saying but it can interpret and remember sounds and tones of voice.

Never bully your dog by shouting at it or hitting it. If you catch it in the act of behaving badly tell it off in a stern voice. But if it behaves well, reward it with warm praise. Your dog will respond to you by remembering to do the things for which it is praised.

Best of all, if you want to train your dog thoroughly, seek out a dog training class – with a trainer that only uses non-violent methods.

A well-trained dog will obey you all the time – even when it is playing.

BODY LANGUAGE

A dog shows how it feels by the position of its body. Here are some common body postures.

Alert and confident. The body is held firm, with head up. The tail is probably wagging.

Apologetic. If a dog is frightened of you it will probably adopt this position.

Playful. Crouching, ears up, tail wagging. This happy dog wants to play.

Afraid. The tail falls between the legs, the body is held low and the head is level with the back.

Wanting. A dog may do this when it would like something from you, such as affection or food.

Submissive. This frightened dog has given in completely. There is no greater sign of submission than this.

DOG OWNER'S CODE

- Train your dog. For best results, take your pet to obedience classes.
- Don't frighten, bully or hit your dog.
- Keep a collar with an identity tag on your dog.
- Control your dog at all times.
- Keep your dog on a lead near roads or farms.
- Regular exercise is vital.
- When exercising your dog, always take a poop scoop.
- Always dispose of your dog's mess properly.
- Give your dog its own bed.
- Feed your dog at the same time every day.
- Feed your dog from its own bowl.
- Keep your dog clean.
- Don't let your dog disturb other people.
- Don't let your dog wander off on its own.
- Register your dog with a vet.

USEFUL WORDS

Beard – thick hair on muzzle and chin.

Bat ears – broad, upright ears with round tips.

Bitch – female dog.

Blaze – white marking up face and between eyes.

Coursing – chasing game animals (usually hares) for sport.

Cropped ears – ears with hanging part removed.

Docked tail – tail that has had end removed.

Feathering – long fringe of hair.

Game – animals hunted for sport, such as birds, hares and rabbits.

Mask – dark colour on muzzle.

Muzzle – snout, including mouth and nose.

Pests – animal considered destructive and harmful.

Ruff – thick hair around neck.

Toy – very small breed.

Undercoat – soft, furry hair under outer hair of some breeds.

WEß SITES

If you have access to the Internet, you will be able to find out lots more about dogs online. Here are some Web sites to visit:

GENERAL

An alphabetical guide to dog breeds, including lots of pictures.

www.dogbreedinfo.com/

Two sites that give current news and general information about dog-related matters.

www.dog.com/

www.dogsworldwide.com/

Comprehensive medical and behavioural information for dog owners. (Note: if your dog appears ill, take it to a vet. Do not try to treat it yourself following a home diagnosis.)

www.vetinfo.com/doginfo.html

Crufts, Europe's premier dog annual dog show.

www.crufts.org.uk

The National Dog Championships, held annually in the USA.

www.newportdogshows.com/nds-ndc1.htm

ANIMAL WELFARE

Sites devoted to the relief of animal suffering.

Australia
www.animalwelfareleague.com.au

Canada
www.cfhs.ca

New Zealand
www.rspcanz.org.nz

UK
www.rspca.org/

www.ncdl.org.uk

USA
www.animalwelfareleague.com/

KENNEL CLUBS

Registrars of dog breeds, and information sources for dog enthusiasts.

Australia
www.ankc.aust.com

Canada
www.ckc.ca

New Zealand
www.nzkc.org.nz

UK
www.the-kennel-club.org.uk

USA
www.akc.org

Continental Kennel Club
www.ckcusa.com

National Kennel Club
www.nationalkennelclub.com

SPOTTER'S CHART

The dogs on this chart are arranged in alphabetical order. When you see one, write down the date you spotted it in the space next to the name.

Name of breed	Date	Name of breed	Date
Affenpinscher		Elkhound	
Alaskan Malamute		Foxhound	
Anatolian Karabash		German Shepherd Dog	
Basenji		Great Dane	
Basset Griffon Vendéen		Greyhound	
Beagle		Greyhound, Italian	
Bichon Frise		Griffon Brabançon	
Bloodhound		Griffon Bruxellois	
Borzoi		Groenendael	
Bouvier des Flandres		Hound, Afghan	
Boxer		Hound, Basset	
Briard		Hound, Ibizan	
Bulldog		Hound, Pharaoh	
Bulldog, French		Husky, Siberian	
Bullmastiff		Japanese Chin	
Cattle Dog, Australian		Keeshond	
Chihuahua, Long-coat		Kelpie	
Chihuahua, Smooth-coat		Komondor	
Chinese Crested Dog		Kuvasz	
Chow Chow		Leonberger	
Collie, Bearded		Lhasa Apso	
Collie, Border		Löwchen	
Collie, Rough		Lurcher	
Collie, Smooth		Malinois	
Corgi, Cardigan		Maltese	
Corgi, Pembroke		Maremma	
Dachshund, Long-haired		Mountain Dog, Bernese	
Dachshund, Smooth-haired		Mountain Dog, Estrela	
Dachshund, Wire-haired		Mountain Dog, Pyrenean	
Dalmatian		Münsterlander, Large	
Deerhound		Münsterlander, Small	
Dobermann		Newfoundland	
Drentse Patrijshond		Norwegian Buhund	

Name of breed	Date	Name of breed	Date
Otterhound		Spaniel, King Charles	
Papillon		Spaniel, Sussex	
Pekingese		Spaniel, Tibetan	
Pinscher, Miniature		Spaniel, Welsh Springer	
Pointer		Spitz, Finnish	
Pointer, German, Short-haired		Terrier, Airedale	
Pomeranian		Terrier, Australian	
Poodle, Miniature		Terrier, Australian Silky	
Poodle, Standard		Terrier, Bedlington	
Poodle, Toy		Terrier, Border	
Pug		Terrier, Boston	
Puli		Terrier, Bull	
Retriever, Chesapeake Bay		Terrier, Cairn	
Retriever, Curly-coated		Terrier, Dandie Dinmont	
Retriever, Flat-coated		Terrier, English Toy	
Retriever, Golden		Terrier, Fox, Smooth-coat	
Retriever, Labrador		Terrier, Fox, Wire-coat	
Rhodesian Ridgeback		Terrier, Irish	
Rottweiler		Terrier, Jack Russell	
St Bernard		Terrier, Kerry Blue	
Saluki		Terrier, Lakeland	
Samoyed		Terrier, Manchester	
Schipperke		Terrier, Norfolk	
Schnauzer, Giant		Terrier, Norwich	
Schnauzer, Miniature		Terrier, Scottish	
Schnauzer, Standard		Terrier, Sealyham	
Setter, English		Terrier, Staffordshire Bull	
Setter, Gordon		Terrier, Tibetan	
Setter, Irish		Terrier, Welsh	
Sheepdog, Old English		Terrier, West Highland	
Sheepdog, Shetland		Terrier, Yorkshire	
Shih Tzu		Tervueren	
Sloughi		Vallhund	
Spaniel, American Cocker		Vizsla	
Spaniel, Brittany		Weimeraner	
Spaniel, Cavalier King Charles		Whippet	
Spaniel, Clumber		Wolfhound, Irish	
Spaniel, Cocker			
Spaniel, English Springer			
Spaniel, Field			
Spaniel, Irish Water			

INDEX OF BREEDS